The text in this edition of *Baby Bear, Baby Bear,*
What Do You See? has been reformatted for beginning readers.

Author's Note
North America is filled with thousands of species of wildlife. These creatures have lived in
their habitats for centuries. Together, we can work to ensure that they will remain wild and
free forever. This book features ten of these great American animals.

The author wishes to thank Michael Sampson for his help in the preparation of this text.

The Eric Carle Museum of Picture Book Art was built to celebrate
the art that we are first exposed to as children. Located in Amherst,
Massachusetts, the 40,000-square-foot museum is the first in the
United States devoted to national and international picture book art.

Visit www.carlemuseum.org

Visit mackids.com/series/MyFirstReader/BillMartinJr
to learn about Bill Martin Jr's approach to reading.

Henry Holt and Company, LLC
Publishers since 1866
175 Fifth Avenue
New York, New York 10010
mackids.com

Henry Holt® is a registered trademark of Henry Holt and Company, LLC.
Text copyright © 2007 by the Estate of Bill Martin Jr
Illustrations copyright © 2007 by Eric Carle
Additional material copyright © 2011 by Henry Holt and Company, LLC
All rights reserved.

Library of Congress Cataloging-in-Publication Data
Martin, Bill, 1916-2004.
Baby bear, baby bear, what do you see? / by Bill Martin Jr. ; pictures by Eric Carle.
p.   cm. — (My first reader)
Summary: Illustrations and rhyming text portray a young bear searching for its mother
and meeting many North American animals along the way in this easy-reader version
of the 2007 tale. Includes note to parents and teachers, as well as activities.
ISBN 978-0-8050-9291-2 (paper over board : alk. paper)
[1. Stories in rhyme. 2. Bears—Fiction. 3. Mother and child—Fiction.
4. Animals—Fiction.] I. Carle, Eric, ill. II. Title.
PZ8.3.M418Bab 2011   [E]—dc22   2010011693

First hardcover edition—2007
First My First Reader edition—2011
Printed in China by South China Printing Company Ltd., Dongguan City, Guangdong Province

10 9 8 7 6 5 4 3 2

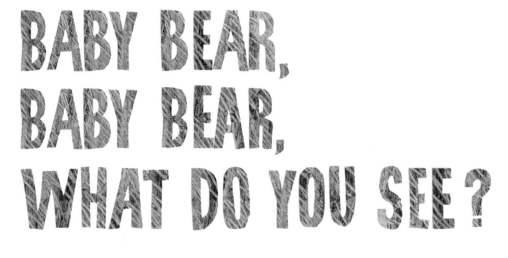

BABY BEAR, BABY BEAR, WHAT DO YOU SEE?

By Bill Martin Jr
Pictures by Eric Carle

Henry Holt and Company · New York

Baby Bear,
Baby Bear,
what do you see?

I see a red fox
slipping by me.

Red Fox,
Red Fox,
what do you see?

I see a flying squirrel
gliding by me.

6

Flying Squirrel,
Flying Squirrel,
what do you see?

I see a mountain goat
climbing near me.

Mountain Goat,
Mountain Goat,
what do you see?

I see a blue heron
flying by me.

Blue Heron,
Blue Heron,
what do you see?

11

I see a prairie dog
digging by me.

12

Prairie Dog,
Prairie Dog,
what do you see?

I see a striped skunk
strutting by me.

Striped Skunk,
Striped Skunk,
what do you see?

15

I see a mule deer
running by me.

Mule Deer,
Mule Deer,
what do you see?

I see a rattlesnake
sliding by me.

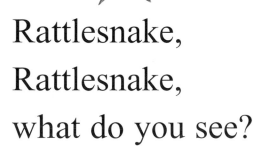

Rattlesnake,
Rattlesnake,
what do you see?

I see a screech owl
hooting at me.

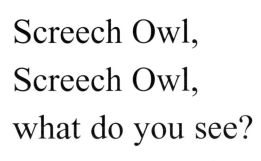

Screech Owl,
Screech Owl,
what do you see?

21

I see a mama bear
looking at me.

Mama Bear,
Mama Bear,
what do you see?

I see…

a red fox,   a flying squirrel,

a prairie dog,   a striped skunk,

a screech owl and…

a mountain goat,   a blue heron,

a mule deer,   a rattlesnake,

my baby bear
looking at me—
that's what I see.

25

DEAR PARENTS AND TEACHERS,

Baby Bear, Baby Bear, What Do You See? is a patterned, question-and-answer book. These qualities can be helpful to children learning to read because the repetitive language along with word clues in Eric Carle's pictures help children to predict what happens next, to remember the story, and to learn to read many of the words easily.

Here are some ways that you might use this book with children:

- ✦ Before opening the book, talk about the bears on the cover. Ask, "What might Baby Bear see?"
- ✦ Next, turn the pages and enjoy the bold collage art together. Ask, "What do you know about this animal?"
- ✦ After you read and reread the story many times, pause before an animal or an action word and encourage your child to supply that word. If your child doesn't chime in, try again on another day.
- ✦ See the following pages for more activities.

When your child says, "I want to read this book by myself!" celebrate the reading and listen with enthusiasm as your child reads it again and again.

—LAURA ROBB
EDUCATOR AND READING CONSULTANT

What animal names
can you read?

red fox

flying squirrel

mountain goat

blue heron

prairie dog

Can you match the words
to the pictures?

striped skunk

mule deer

rattlesnake

screech owl

What action words
can you read?

slip

glide

climb

fly

dig

Can you act
them out?

strut

run

slide

hoot

look

Where do these
animals live?

In the
  ground

On the
  ground

In a tree

How does each
animal move?

Four legs

Two legs

Wings